TROUBLE ON BOARD SHIP!

. . . Basil had been studying maps and charts to determine which island was inhabited by pygmy cats.

"Dawson, it's discouraging! The Captain hasn't heard of such an island, and he knows these seas like the back of his paw. It must be far off the regular shipping lanes. It would take forever to visit all the islands. Some are just tiny pinpoints of land. If only I had a clue!"

"You'll find one," said I. "Sherlock Holmes never fails, and neither will you. Keep at it, and—"

We were interrupted by a terrified young sailor.

"Oh sirs! There's big trouble—I sneaked off before they saw me. Mutiny, that's what it is! They'll throw the Captain overboard unless he tells them the combination of the safe."

BASIL AND THE PYGMY CATS
was originally published by
McGraw-Hill Book Company.

Critics' Corner:

"An archeological mystery leads Basil, the 'Sherlock Holmes of the Mouse World,' and his cohorts from London to the volcanic island of Kataarh in the Orient to untangle the age-old story of pygmy cats. . . . The unearthing of buildings, sculptures, wall paintings, and scrolls is a microcosmic presentation of the archeologist's business, cleverly devised and made entertaining with invented names and strange creatures—such as the sacred catfish that speaks many languages. Equally amusing as the preceding stories . . . with Paul Galdone again adding his humor to the parody." —*Horn Book*

"Fans of the above-stairs inhabitants of Baker Street won't be disappointed, and even younger children who miss the parody will enjoy the ample action." —*Library Journal*

"Wild imagination tempered with pure humor makes this adventure-mystery fun. . . ." —*Los Angeles Times*

Also recommended by: Child Study Association.

About the Author and Illustrator:

EVE TITUS is the author of many children's books, including those about the French cheese-tasting mouse, Anatole. A professional concert-pianist, she has always had two loves, writing and music. Miss Titus originated and personally conducts her Storybook Writing Seminar each summer. Born and raised in New York City, she has lived in Mexico for three years. California is her present home, and summers are spent on a small Greek island, writing and giving her workshop. Of the first *Basil of Baker Street* mystery, Adrian M. Conan Doyle wrote the author, "May I offer you my heartfelt congratulations. It is a simply wonderful creation, and I can assure you that my father would have revelled in every page." *Basil of Baker Street* is also in an Archway Paperback edition.

PAUL GALDONE came to this country from Budapest, Hungary, and studied at the Art Students League in New York. He is a well-known illustrator of children's literature and lives with his wife and their two children in Rockland County, New York.

BASIL

AND THE
PYGMY CATS

BASIL
AND THE
PYGMY CATS

A BASIL OF BAKER STREET MYSTERY

BY EVE TITUS
ILLUSTRATED BY PAUL GALDONE

AN ARCHWAY PAPERBACK
POCKET BOOKS • NEW YORK

BASIL AND THE PYGMY CATS

Archway Paperback edition published August, 1973

L

Published by
POCKET BOOKS, a division of Simon & Schuster, Inc.,
630 Fifth Avenue, New York, N.Y.

Archway Paperback editions are distributed in the U.S.
by Simon & Schuster, Inc., 630 Fifth Avenue, New
York, N.Y. 10020, and in Canada by Simon & Schuster
of Canada, Ltd., Richmond Hill, Ontario, Canada.

TO THE ADMIRABLE
ADRIAN M. CONAN DOYLE
and to his amazing
Sherlock Holmes Museum
in Lucens Castle,
Switzerland

Cast of Characters

BASIL	*an English mouse detective*
DR. DAWSON	*his friend and associate*
MRS. JUDSON	*their mousekeeper*
CYRIL	*a stoolpigeon*
DR. SINGH LHA	*a mouse with a clue*
PROFESSOR RATIGAN	*arch villain*
CAPTAIN DORAN	*the villain's aide*
MLLE. RELDA	*a mouse opera star*
GENERAL GARMIZE	*a French military mouse*

THE MAHARAJAH OF BENGISTAN

an Oriental ruler

CAPTAIN PETER BLACK *a British seamouse*

JEANNIE *a two-headed sea monster*

THE SACRED CATFISH *who speaks seven*

languages

KAHLÚA *chief of the pygmy cats*

LORD ADRIAN

ANTOINE CHERBOU

DR. ARTHUR HOWARD *mouse members*

TILLARY QUINN *of the expedition*

YOUNG RICHARD *(alphabetically)*

VINCENZO STARRETTI

DR. JULIAN WOLFF

ORIENTAL MICE GANGSTERS SAILORS

PYGMY CATS BRITISH CATS

(and a cast of thousands)

Contents

BASIL
AND THE
PYGMY CATS

1

The Clue of
the Golden Goblet

Pygmy Cats! Breathes there, in all the world, a mouse who is not stirred by those two words?

Did the miniature monsters actually exist? Our leading mouse scientists were not certain, but they all believed the answer would be found in the Orient.

It was Basil of Baker Street, the Sherlock Holmes of the Mouse World, who solved the mystery. He used his skill as a scientific sleuth to bring to light secrets long hidden behind the curtains of the past, secrets no other mouse had been able to discover.

Professor Ratigan, leader of the mouse underworld, stalked him at every turn! Danger was Basil's constant companion. Ratigan's spies were at the border, in the jungle, on the ship, and—

But let me tell you how the adventure began. . . .

The year is 1894. The place is London,

England, at Baker Street, Number 221,B, where live Mr. Sherlock Holmes and his friend, Dr. John H. Watson.

Mr. Holmes is the World's Greatest Human Detective. Basil is the World's Greatest Mouse Detective, and I, Dr. David Q. Dawson, am his friend.

We dwell in the cellar of 221,B, in the mouse town of Holmestead, which Basil named after his hero. My friend would often scurry up secret passageways to Mr. Holmes' rooms. There he would take notes in short-paw as the human detective told Dr. Watson exactly how he solved his difficult cases. One might say that Basil studied at the great man's feet.

Did Mr. Holmes ever see his small admirer, hidden in a corner? I believe he did, and that it pleased him to pass his methods on to a mouse.

And *such* a mouse! I am of average height, about five inches tall, but Basil towers a full inch above me.

My notebook is crammed with accounts of

his cases. I am a busy doctor, but whenever possible, I take pen in paw to write of his achievements. Would that I had time to narrate them all!

There was the Mystery of the Bald-headed Mouse, a bank director. One foggy morning he stepped out of his office and vanished, along with a lot of the bank's money. Mouseland Yard detectives sought him with no success, but Basil studied the clues and found the bald banker in Edinburgh, wearing a wig and using another name. Most of the stolen funds were untouched, for spending large sums in Scotland would have drawn attention to the thief at once.

Then there was the Case of the Guinea-Pig Gang. The honest mice of London dared not venture out at night until Basil cleverly found the criminals' hideout and had them all jailed.

But of all his cases, Basil's own favorite is the Adventure of the Pygmy Cats. It put to use all his remarkable skill as a sleuth, plus his vast knowledge of the science of archeology.

Basil's hobby was archeology. He had discovered Rockhenge, the ancient mouse ruins near London.

Interviewed by newspapermice, Basil said, "The most exciting detective work in the world is archeology! As we dig, clues keep turning up. Arrowheads, old weapons, broken bowls—any or all may hold clues to the life and times of prehistoric mice. The calendar stone I found at Rockhenge, for example, proved that mice perfected a 365-day calendar long before mankind. Clearly, archeology is the highest form of detective work, for lessons we learn from the past help mice to build a better, brighter future!"

The clues concerning the pygmy cats were to take us halfway across the world, to the Far East.

Originally we had planned our trip to the Orient for a different reason—to restore the Maharajah of Bengistan to his rightful throne.

Cyril the Stoolpigeon had brought word that our enemy, Professor Ratigan, now ruled Bengistan, a mouse kingdom near India.

Too large to enter, the pigeon stood at our window to tell us what a little Oriental bird had told him.

In a surprise move the Professor and his gang had stormed and taken the palace. They guarded the border day and night. The Maharajah was unharmed, but kept prisoner in his private apartments in the palace. Ratigan taxed everything, even cheese! Mice too poor to pay the tax starved. And all the tax money went into Ratigan's pockets!

"Thank you, Cyril," said Basil. "You may pick up your reward at the back window. Mrs. Judson, our mousekeeper, baked blackberry tarts today."

Cyril, grinning happily, was off in a trice.

Basil's eyes blazed. "That rat Ratigan! Robbing our friend of his throne! I cannot stand idly by—we leave for the Orient at dawn. Can you arrange to have another doctor attend your patients?"

I could, and did, by nightfall. Then, having packed, we relaxed in easy chairs before the fire.

The doorbell jangled, and Mrs. Judson ushered in Dr. Edward Hagerup, a Norwegian scientist from the British Mousmopolitan Museum.

After we all shook paws, he held up a golden goblet of ancient design. I reproduce it below.

Basil studied the goblet, and chuckled. "My word! Elotana, Goddess of Goodness! European mice worshipped her thousands of years ago. Look—kneeling before her are

Oriental-looking pygmy cats scarcely the size of mice! Where was the goblet found?"

"In Turkey," said Hagerup. "It proves that pygmy cats existed. We of the Mousmopolitan know you are going to the Orient. We feel you are the only mouse who can solve this mystery. Will you try?"

Basil nodded. "Gladly, after I've captured Ratigan. A noted archeologist once said, 'One pits one's wits against the past!' How true! This will be the most challenging case of my career!"

Quickly Basil sketched the scene on the goblet, and the Norwegian departed with the original.

That night scores of midget cats marched through my slumbers, shaking with fright at sight of me. Seldom have I enjoyed more delightful dreams!

2

Off to the Orient!

At dawn London was blanketed by fog, and we could scarcely see our paws before our faces. By stealing rides, we reached Dover, then crossed the English Channel as stowaways on a steamer.

In France we boarded the boat-train for Paris, arriving in a downpour. Soaked to the fur, we called on Inspector Antoine Cherbou of the policemice.

Told of our mission, the Inspector arranged to join us, along with the famous General Garmize.

When the Simplon Express left Paris that night, four mice were aboard. Carrier pigeons had spread news of our plans, and as we sped across Europe on one crack express train after another, many well-known mice joined our party.

Our accommodations were often luxuri-

ous, but whenever people entered, we had to scamper off to the baggage car.

Lord Adrian, historian of the International Society of Mouse Mountaineers, boarded at Geneva. He was a famed hunter of sharks, those horrors of the deep. With him came Tillary Quinn, author and adventurer, Dr. Arthur Howard, a geologist, and Dr. Julian Wolff, a medical mouse. And so it went, until our party numbered twenty.

One night we reached Turkey. All were

asleep but Basil and myself, and we stepped out for some air.

Waiting on the platform were Young Richard, an American scientist, and the archeologist Dr. Singh Lha. Two Turkish workmice stood behind them, bearing a large, bulky object. They unwrapped it to reveal a painted vase.

"A clue to the pygmy cats!" said Dr. Lha. "It was found on a site I am excavating, here in Turkey!"

"Amazing! Astounding! Astonishing!" cried Basil. "Painted here are pygmy cats in Oriental robes and turbans, carrying bamboo chairs in which sit King Elyod and Queen Nairda, mouse rulers of ancient times. But Elyod and Nairda were Europeans, not Orientals—how strange!"

I, too, was mystified. Every schoolmouse knew of Elyod the Good. About two thousand years ago he had ruled Euphoria, a mouse kingdom near Athens, Greece. His court had been a center of learning, where all the great mouse minds of the time gathered.

Ancient Euphorians had also been explorers and traders, sailing far in their sturdy little ships.

One day Elyod set sail, seeking a short route to India. Sixty mice embarked—the King's son, Semloh the Poet Prince, the Queen, and many nobles.

Cheering throngs lined the waterfront to wave farewell to their beloved rulers. Alas,

14

the farewells were final—of all who sailed that fateful day, not one mouse returned!

Historians believed that a violent storm had wrecked the ship and drowned everyone aboard.

Basil's voice broke into my thoughts. "Can it be that the mice did not drown, but were cast ashore on an island in the Indian Ocean?"

He paced to and fro, thinking deeply.

"Suppose that pygmy cats lived on the island, cats who had never seen mice. Would they not have welcomed the castaways? As for King Elyod, an island paradise is every mouse's dream, and there was a challenge, too—could mice rule cats? Elyod took up that challenge. The painting on the vase proves it. But why was the vase discovered in Turkey, in the Near East, so far from the Far East?"

He gripped Singh Lha's paw. "Thanks for bringing the vase—I've memorized the painting. If I solve the mystery surrounding Elyod

15

and the pygmy cats, cat and mouse history will be rewritten!"

The train moved slowly, then picked up speed.

Waving to Singh Lha, Basil, Young Richard, and I swung aboard.

3

In the Dungeon

Two days later we left the train. Hitching rides, we crossed southern India, headed toward Bengistan. Jolting rides on rutted roads jarred our spines, and we longed for the plush comfort of the trains.

However, we found compensation in scenic beauties—the mountains, the verdant valleys, the vivid hues of the tropics.

Sprawled in the back of an oxcart one day,

we sang, all but Basil, who sat alone, deep in thought.

Vincenzo Starretti conducted us in the Soldiers' Chorus from *Faust*. I must say we sang well, though softly, not wishing to alert the driver to our presence.

Then we began a lusty pirate tune, but there was an interruption.

Basil jumped up, shouting, "Pirates! That's the answer! Turkish pirates, the terror of the seas!"

"You've ruined the music!" said Starretti sternly.

"I'm sorry. The word *pirate* gave me a clue. Elyod wished the world to know he was alive on his island. He had a ship built to replace the wrecked one, and sent captain and crew to Euphoria with the news. He also sent some pretty things made on the island, such as the golden goblet and the vase. But the ship never reached Euphoria, for on the way—"

"Pirates! Turkish pirates!" we all cried.

"Precisely. Their favorite sport was to ram

19

a ship, transfer the cargo to their own ships, and make the captured mice walk the plank. Often they would sink the ship, letting everyone drown!"

"Horrible!" said I. "With Elyod's captain and crew dead, no one knew the King still lived."

"As for the vase found in Turkey," said Basil, "pirates often hid their loot inland and then forgot where. But where is the Island of Pygmy Cats?"

Lord Adrian's eyes twinkled. "If all cats were pygmies, this world would be a better place!"

"Hear, hear!" we cried, but Young Richard, who had been studying his maps, pointed to the road.

"Our jumping-off spot! Beyond it—Bengistan!"

We left the lumbering oxcart and plunged into the underbrush. Bumpy roads were bad, but dense jungle was worse. The going was rough, with grass and roots so thick that we had to use our axes.

At nightfall we heard the eerie calls and whoops of birds, and dared not light our lanterns. Some of the birds might be fond of mice—*too* fond! But luck was with us that long night—no one was eaten.

At dawn, near the border of Bengistan, Basil appointed Cherbou and General Garmize leaders of two groups. They were to find an unguarded place.

"Once over the border," said Basil, "you must organize the native mice. They all hate Ratigan for holding their Maharajah hostage. Dawson and I will let ourselves be captured. We'll probably be prisoners in the palace, where I'll find a way to rescue the Maharajah. When next we meet, Bengistan shall be free. Good-bye and good luck!"

All went as planned. Basil and I were arrested at the border. Captain Doran, a London criminal, recognized us at once.

"What a catch!" he sneered. "The great detective, Basil of Baker Street, and his friend Dawson! Guards, take them to the palace!"

We were prodded along at bayonet point and then flung into one of the palace dungeons, as dark and dismal a place as ever I'd seen, lit by one candle.

"We'll be having a visitor soon," said Basil, and he was right. Half an hour later the rusty iron door clanged open.

A tall, stoop-shouldered mouse entered, wearing a crown—Ratigan, the brains of the mouse underworld!

The brilliant criminal smiled mockingly as he faced the famous detective.

"When last we met, you were the victor, Basil. Now the tables are turned! It's King Ratigan, who rules, and you, the champion of law and order, who's the loser. Haven't you learned your lesson yet? Join up with me, Basil! I admire your great mental powers and your genius as a detective. If you and I should pool our brains, we'd rule the entire mouse world. What do you say?"

"Never!" cried my friend. "My whole life is dedicated to fighting the evil for which you stand. I'll do my best to put you and your gang in jail for the rest of your lives!"

Ratigan's smile vanished. "You'll regret those words, Basil of Baker Street. For all I care, you can rot in this dungeon forever!"

Glaring angrily, he turned on his heel and left.

4

The Tunnel

No sooner had the sound of Ratigan's steps died away than Basil whipped out his magnifying glass and began exploring the dungeon, candle held high. The floor and the walls were of large blocks of stone, and he inspected them carefully.

I stretched out on some straw in the corner, but just as my eyes closed, Basil called, "Dawson! There's a message scratched on the wall, high above my head. Let me stand on your shoulders."

Yawning, I obliged. Basil copied the message in his notebook and jumped down. He studied the writing for a few minutes, then exclaimed aloud in satisfaction. Thrusting the message under my nose, he commanded me to read it.

I stared at this puzzling jumble of letters:

TJYUI SPX   GPVSUI TUPOF   UVOOFM

"My mind's a blank," said I. "What does it mean?"

"I'll give you a hint," replied Basil. "It's in English, the second language of Bengistan, and it's in an alphabet code."

I sighed. "It might as well be in Martian!"

"Heavens, Dawson! It's a simple code in which the letters of the alphabet are moved to the left. Here's my notebook—print the alphabet under the message and decipher it."

I obeyed and found myself studying the following:

TJYUI SPX GPVSUI TUPOF UVOOFM
ABCDEFGHIJKLMNOPQRSTUVWXYZ

"Let me see," said I. "T moved to the left becomes s, J becomes I, Y becomes x, U becomes T, and I is now H. By Jove! TJYUI stands for SIXTH!"

"Elementary, my dear doctor. Pray continue."

I quickly decoded the rest and read the message!"

SIXTH ROW FOURTH STONE TUNNEL

Highly excited, we began counting stones. The fourth stone in the sixth row was loose! We pried it up, using my walking-stick as a lever. Basil dropped down into the tunnel, then steadied the stone as I jumped. We eased it back into place to hide our way of escape.

Then we began to crawl along, taking turns at holding the candle. The ceiling of the tunnel was so low that we could hardly

lift our heads for fear of bumping ourselves. Several times the candle sputtered and went out, leaving us in complete darkness. I must confess to feelings of panic until the candle was lit again, for the air was foul and oppressive, and I kept asking myself—what if the tunnel ends in a blank wall? Twice I thought of returning to the dungeon, but Basil continued to creep forward, and I followed his brave example.

Suddenly the narrow tunnel began slanting

upward. Now it was even more difficult to go on. We inched along at a snail's pace, with myself in the lead.

Suddenly I banged my head against something and had to halt.

"Ouch!" I cried, but Basil put his paw to his lips, cautioning silence. He held the flickering candle a little higher. The passage ended there—straight ahead was a wooden panel. Would it open, I wondered, or was it a dead end?

Basil inspected the panel with his magnifying lens as well as he could from his crouching position.

"The panel will swing open," he whispered, his face grim. "However, we are in deadly peril, for we have no way of knowing who lurks on the other side—friends or foes!"

5

The Mob Marches!

Gently Basil pushed against the panel. It swung inward, revealing a spacious room, luxuriously furnished. And luck was with us again—there, seated at a desk, head bowed in deep despair, was our good friend the Maharajah.

Noiselessly we slid into the room. Then Basil sauntered over to the desk and said, "The Maharajah of Bengistan, I presume?"

Our friend looked up, and with a glad cry sprang from his chair.

"I had a premonition that you would come, Basil. Many's the scrape you rescued me from in our college days! But how on earth did you get here?"

Our story was soon told, and the Maharajah said, "Bless the mouse who built that secret panel, whoever he was! I never knew the panel existed. Now we must act fast—the Professor is in the music-salon, listening to Relda sing, as he does each afternoon at five."

"Mlle. Relda—here?" I asked in surprise.

"Yes, Dawson. She was giving a song recital in the palace when Ratigan took over, and became his prisoner. He is passionately fond of opera, and so she has to sing arias for him every day. At first she refused, but two days without any food made her change her mind."

"That beast!" said Basil grimly. "Now I've another score to settle with the Professor, for

he knows how we all adore the lovely singer.
If he has harmed one hair of her head, I'll—"

"Less words and more action," said the
Maharajah quietly, and Basil agreed.

He fitted a master key to the lock of a
great oaken door, and quickly opened it.

Stealthily we entered the music-salon
through the back door. The lovely Relda stood
on a small stage at the front, singing the Mad
Scene from *Lucia di Lammermoor*. Ratigan
sat listening, so entranced by the clear, soar-

ing soprano voice that we took him completely by surprise, and bound and gagged him.

Relda was overcome by joy, and thanked us over and over again.

Then Basil addressed the Professor, saying, "Turnabout is fair play, Ratigan. You rule no more! In fact, my dear ex-king, you shall soon see the inside of a dungeon, just as Dawson and I did. May you enjoy the Maharajah's hospitality! Moreover, the others of my expedition must have carried out my plans, for

32

if I mistake not, at this very moment I hear a welcome sound—the mob marches!"

We stepped out on the balcony. Through the palace gates strode General Garmize, waving his sword. Hundreds of loyal mice marched behind him.

"Down with Ratigan! Long live the Maharajah!" they shouted, and stormed the palace.

It was all over quickly. The gangsters threw down their weapons, begging for mercy, and were hurled into dungeons. Unfortunately, the Professor and Doran were put into the same dungeon Basil and I had occupied. Ratigan found the loose stone and the two scoundrels escaped.

But we did not know of this as we stood on the balcony and heard his Highness say, "My good and loyal subjects, meet the mastermind who saved my kingdom—Basil of Baker Street!"

The cheers for Basil were absolutely deafening.

A banquet was held in the palace in our honor, with rare Oriental cheeses and veiled dancing-mice.

While we all watched the swaying dancers, Basil told the Maharajah about the pygmy cats, and was promised a two-masted schooner, complete with captain and crew.

At last we would start on our quest!

6

Mutiny!

It was our second afternoon aboard ship.

I stood at the rail of the yacht *Rosetta,* enchanted by the beauty around me—the turquoise sea, the pale blue of the sky, the swirling white spray in our wake as the ship skimmed over the waters.

The elegant *Rosetta* was a two-masted schooner of modern design, with auxiliary motors for emergencies. There were a dozen double-sized passenger cabins, plus captain's quarters, officers' quarters, and space for crew. In the forecastle was the galley, or kitchen, where ship's cooks prepared tasty meals.

The Maharajah had stayed behind to put his kingdom in order. General Garmize, whose cousin Jacques Bernard taught French at the palace, had remained to train the army.

Captain Peter Black, a jolly Britisher, told me his crew was Bengistanian, all but two new sailors.

I had seen the pair—surly fellows who never smiled. One of them wore a black eye-patch.

Basil had been studying maps and charts to determine which island was inhabited by pygmy cats.

"Dawson, it's discouraging! The Captain hasn't heard of such an island, and he knows these seas like the back of his paw. It must be far off the regular shipping lanes. It would take forever to visit all the islands. Some are just tiny pinpoints of land. If only I had a clue!"

"You'll find one," said I. "Sherlock Holmes never fails, and neither will you. Keep at it, and—"

We were interrupted by a terrified young sailor.

"Oh sirs! There's big trouble—I sneaked off before they saw me. Mutiny, that's what it is! They'll throw the Captain overboard unless he tells them the combination of the safe."

"Who are the mutineers?" asked the detective.

"The new sailors, Nagitar and Narod," was the reply.

Basil's eyes glittered. "What's that you say? *Nagitar and Narod?* Incredible! I shall confront the mutineers, but first bring me a large sheet of paper and a black crayon."

The sailor obeyed. Basil crayoned something on the paper, and we tiptoed to the top deck.

The Captain was tied up, and the sailors

were herded against the rail, kept there at gunpoint by the two mutineers.

The mouse with the eye-patch spoke to the crew.

"We'll divide the money in the safe. Then, with me as your captain, we'll become smugglers."

"But Captain Black is always kind to us," said a sailor. "Why should we mutiny against him?"

The pair had their backs to us; the crew faced us.

"Dawson, draw your gun," whispered Basil. "Cover Nagitar, who wears the black eye-patch."

I edged over and jabbed my gun into the ruffian's back. "One move and you're a dead mouse!" I said.

Basil stood beside me, holding the paper high.

"Bengistanians!" he called. "Who robbed your Maharajah of his throne? Who looted your country?"

"Ratigan!" they screamed. "And Doran!"

"Right!" declared Basil. "Now read the names on this paper backward, and you'll learn the *real* names of the mutineers."

The sailors read the names and surged forward, faces furious, crying out for revenge. Ratigan and Doran were overpowered and taken prisoner.

We freed the Captain, who ordered a lifeboat loaded with enough food and water for a few days.

NAGITAR
NAROD

"Ratigan and Doran, you deserve to be thrown overboard!" said Captain Black. "Instead, two of my sailors will row you back to Bengistan to stand trial."

"And after you serve your sentence," added Basil, "the policemice of London will be glad to give you free lodging in an English jail."

Ratigan's face twisted with rage. "Don't count on it, Basil of Baker Street! I'll foil you yet!"

(We learned later of his escape. Doran gnawed at Ratigan's ropes in the dark. Freeing themselves, the two criminals tied up the sailors and landed at night without being caught. Returning to London, they reorganized their gangs.)

Unaware that this would occur, I watched the lifeboat vanish from view. The others went below, and once again I stood alone at the rail.

Suddenly I blinked in stunned surprise—two snakelike heads were rising from the sea! The heads rose higher, followed by two long necks.

Imagine my horror to see that the two necks were joined together, were one!

"It's a two-headed sea monster!" I gasped weakly.

Dizziness overcame me, and I fainted dead away!

7

The Two-headed
Sea Monster

A pail of cold water dashed in my face revived me, and Captain Black helped me to my feet.

"I hope you're feeling better," he said. "Cold water may be old-fashioned, but it does the job."

"B-but b-but the m-m-m-monster!" I stammered, turning to where I had last seen it.

To my surprise, it was still there, talking to

Basil, who stood at the rail as though he hadn't a care in the world.

"Save yourself!" I screamed.

But Basil turned and said, "My dear doctor, you've hurt Jeannie's feelings. She hails from Scotland, and the Loch Ness Monster is her uncle. Do come and be introduced—she's really a dear."

"It's a pleasure to meet you," I said politely.

"And I'm *so* glad to meet a doctor," she said. "I feel simply miserable, for one of my heads has a cold. Do you have any medicine for a head cold?"

One face had a sunny smile. The other, with red-rimmed eyes and runny nose, looked glum and gloomy.

I fetched my little black bag, and from it took a large bottle containing a good medicine for colds.

"Jeannie, a mouse needs just a teaspoonful, but a big creature like yourself needs an entire bottle. Now open your mouth and close your eyes!"

She obeyed, lowering the head with the cold to the deck of our ship. I stood halfway up a ladder and poured the bottleful of medicine down her throat.

"Good girl!" I said, mounting to the top of the ladder to pat the top of her head.

She thanked me, then told us her strange story.

(Jeannie had one throat, from which her voice came, but each head had its own mouth. When she spoke, it was most amusing to see two pairs of lips making exactly the same motions. Extraordinary creature!)

"Last year," said she, "our family of Loch Ness monsters traveled around the world. Underwater, of course. I took a wrong turn in the Bay of Bengal, lost the others, and here I am in the Indian Ocean. Oriental monsters, to be sure, are friendly, but I do miss bonnie Scotland and my own dear family. 'Tis homesick I am, such a long way from home.

"But enough about me! Dear little mice, I'm thankful to you all. May I help *you* in any way?"

"We seek an island inhabited by pygmy cats," said Basil. "Do you know of such an island?"

Her two heads moved sadly from side to side.

"Alas, I do not, but I *do* know of someone wondrous wise—the Sacred Catfish. He speaks seven languages and lives in a pond on an island. I'll be glad to show you the way."

Jeannie swam slowly so that our little ship could keep up with her, and presently she stopped.

"I'll wait here in deep water," she said. "Row to the nearest island and look for a pond. Good luck!"

Four of us got into a lifeboat. Cherbou and I rowed, while Basil and Lord Adrian talked about catfish.

"Most fish are covered with scales," said Basil, "but catfish and sharks have smooth skins."

"True," said Lord Adrian. "In Egypt I saw the electric catfish of the River Nile. Its body organs produce enough current to shock a human being. Let's hope the Sacred Catfish won't shock us!"

"We shall soon see for ourselves," answered Basil as we beached the boat and went ashore.

8

The Sacred Catfish

A short walk brought us to the pond. Basil
threw pebbles into it to lure the catfish to the
surface, and soon a huge head appeared.

Ugh! The head was quite large and, to us,
revoltingly ugly, for it strongly resembled the
head of an English tomcat. I noted the big,
wide mouth, the great staring eyes. The bar-
bels, four at each side of the nostrils, looked
like cats' whiskers.

"Species *bagarius yarrelli*," whispered Basil. "Non-electric. Eel-like body may attain a length of six feet. Adapts to marshes and muddy waters."

"Who wishes to consult the Sacred Catfish?" asked a deep, solemn voice in flawless English.

"Basil of Baker Street," calmly replied my friend.

"Ah! The Sherlock Holmes of the Mouse World! You are reputed to be brilliant in many fields. What do you say to a few tests of your knowledge?"

"Fire away!" said Basil. "I'll test yours, too."

The catfish grinned. "Many words start with *cat,* a syllable shunned by mice. Define *category*."

"A *category* is a classification of ideas or things," said Basil. "Your turn—what is a *catalog?*"

"A list of items, often arranged alphabetically, in booklet form. What's a *catboat,* Basil?"

"A one-masted boat with a single sail," said my friend. "Where are Catania and Catanzaro?"

"Catania is in Sicily, Catanzaro in Italy. Where is the Catawba River, Basil?"

"In North Carolina, U.S.A. *Catawba* is also a variety of grape. Tell me, what is *catopsis?*"

"Unusually keen vision. Define *cataphasia*, Basil."

The detective did not hesitate. *"Cataphasia is a speech disorder in which a word or a phrase is constantly repeated, repeated, repeated, repeated—"*

"Touché!" cried the catfish. "Enough! The reports of your brilliance are not exaggerated. Now you may tell me why you came to consult me."

"I seek the Island of the Pygmy Cats," said Basil.

"I'll give you a clue—*think of King Darius!* With your deductive powers the clue should lead to another clue, and then to the island you seek."

Basil bowed. "Sacred Catfish, I thank you. At the moment the clue puzzles me, but no doubt some serious thinking will enlighten me. Before we go, is there anything I can do to repay your kindness?"

"Do you have any catnip?" asked the catfish. "I've heard of this herb but have never tasted it."

"I always carry some for emergencies, and it shall be yours. But I must warn you, Sacred Catfish, that it will turn you—temporarily, of course—into a flighty, foolish creature."

"Basil, we all need some nonsense now and then. I spend all my time thinking deep thoughts and practicing my seven languages. I'd rather like to be silly for a change—temporarily, of course."

"Then so be it," declared Basil, and cast his catnip on the waters.

The catfish nibbled daintily at first. Then, savoring the flavor, he gobbled greedily away.

We soon saw a weird and startling spectacle.

The dignified catfish reared up and stood on his tail, then hopped and skipped and jumped around the pond, talking all the while in his deep voice.

"Fabulous! Fantastic! Such a frightfully funny feeling! Frivol and frolick! Roister and rollick! Such frisky foolery! Such droll folderol!"

The eyes rolled from side to side, the big mouth grinned, the huge body bounced about. At last the effect of the catnip wore off.

"Suddenly I'm sleepy," said the creature. "But before I leave you, I'll prove that I speak seven languages by saying farewell in all seven —French, Spanish, Italian, German, Japanese, Danish, and English ADIEU! ADIÓS! ADDIO! AUF WIEDERSEHEN! SAYONARA! FARVEL! Good-bye!"

The catfish winked at Basil. "Remember King Darius! Not too far away! Farewell, gallant mice!"

And he flipped his tail and sank out of sight.

Basil was silent all the way back to the beach, pondering the problem. We did not interrupt but rowed toward the yacht silently.

Suddenly he cried, "Eureka! I have it! I'll confer with the Captain at once."

When we boarded the yacht, Basil left us.

Young Richard stood on deck, chatting with Jeannie. She was in a happy mood, for she was going home.

"Young Richard is a darling!" she said. "He looked up lots of undersea charts and drew a special diagram for me. I've memorized it."

"She'll be home tomorrow night," said Richard.

"Never had a sense of direction, but my memory's fine," declared Jeannie. "I'll keep looking at the charts in my mind's eye. All of you, be sure to visit me in Scotland and meet my family. 'Bye!"

Smiling two heavenly smiles, and fluttering all her eyelashes, Jeannie submerged, and was gone.

Lord Adrian sighed. "Bonnie lass—we'll miss her winsome ways. Maybe someday we'll visit her."

"What?" said Cherbou. "As guests of the Loch Ness monsters?"

"Why not? Monster is as monster does!"

"Well said!" remarked Basil, who had just come up on deck. "Gather 'round, fellow-mice. I'll tell you the tale of King Darius."

"Man or mouse?" inquired Dr. Wolff, winking broadly.

"Man, Persian. I'm glad he wasn't a Persian cat, for he ruled Persia over two thousand years ago and built up a vast empire. He had the story of his deeds cut into a cliff. On top were huge carved figures of Darius and a few of his subjects."

Basil paused. "The clue the Sacred Catfish gave me was puzzling until I deduced that it must refer to an island with a cliff, one not too far away. Captain Black knows of two such islands nearby, and we're on our way to one right now."

"It seems so simple when you explain your methods," I said. "Yet none of us had any idea of what the clue meant. Basil, you're a wizard!"

He bowed. "I observe, I analyze, I deduce."

When I awoke the next morning, Basil had already left the cabin. I hurried on deck. He stood at the rail and thrust his spyglass at me.

"An amazing view, Dawson. See for yourself!"

Eagerly I peered through the glass. In the distance was a low, grassy island dominated by a steep cliff at one end. On the front face of the cliff I saw a huge stone figure, clearly a mouse, seated on a throne carved into the rock. And beneath the throne was a long inscription!

"Like Darius," said Basil, "King Elyod had his story cut into a cliff. There I hope to find the second clue mentioned by the Sacred Catfish!"

9

The Inscription
on the Cliff

At noon we neared the uninhabited isle.
Captain Black and his crew remained aboard
—the rest of us rowed ashore.

Climbing the front face of the cliff, where
nothing grew, was impossible. Instead, we
climbed a gently sloping path at the back of
the cliff.

At last we reached the top. Palm trees
swayed in the breeze. High above our heads

Elyod's great stone face stared out to sea. Being no bigger than his nose, we felt like midgets!

The inscription went far down the face of the cliff, and I asked Basil how he would read it.

"You'll know tomorrow," he replied. "It's almost dark—let's build a campfire and eat."

Cheese was the starring attraction, not only as food, but as food for thought. That night we shared the cheeses of many nations.

"Behold!" said Starretti. "My music-loving Italian mice sculptured a Provolone cheese, just for me!"

And he unwrapped a cheese shaped like a harp!

After admiring the work of art, we soon disposed of it. The harp strings were most delicious!

Young Richard had Anatolian cheese from Turkey, Cherbou had brought superb Roquefort from France, and Tillary had tangy Bushman cheese, all the way from Australia.

I passed around my Edam, which came

from Holland, and told everyone that it was also called Katzenkopf, or Cat's Head Cheese.

"What's in a name?" asked Lord Adrian. Then he shared his Stilton cheese, remarking, "A bridal cheese made for Queen Victoria weighed more than a thousand pounds!"

"A gift fit for a mouse queen!" said Basil. "In Holland, cats are used to patrol cheese storage caves, because of mice. But the Dutch people *never* throw away a cheese gnawed by mice—they class it as superior!"

Proudly we snuggled into our sleeping bags, and my last thought was—those clever Dutch people!

Early next morning Basil revealed his plan.

"In 1835 an Englishman, Henry Rawlinson, arranged to be lowered from a clifftop in order to copy the Darius inscriptions. I shall do the same."

We were horrified. "Don't do it," I begged. "You could be dashed to death on the rocks below!"

"Is there no other way?" implored Dr.

Wolff. "Mr. Sherlock Holmes himself would mourn your passing."

"It must be done," said Basil, "if we are to find the second clue. But it's better to be safe than sorry. Hollow out half a coconut shell and nail ropes to it. Instead of dangling from a rope, I'll sit in the shell while I copy the inscription."

The coconut was tough, but our axes did the job.

Basil seated himself, and we lowered away. At his cry of "Halt" we tied the rope ends securely to tree trunks.

Then we waited—forever, it seemed. Now and then we heard him call, "A bit lower!" and we obeyed.

Time dragged. I peered down. The heroic mouse sat on his perilous perch, calmly taking notes. Yet at any moment a gust of wind or a belligerent bird could send him spinning downward to his doom.

I trembled and did not look again. Instead, I breathed silent prayers for his safety.

At last came the welcome cry, "Hoist me up!" and we did so, with thanksgiving in our hearts.

Waving his notebook, Basil stepped out of the coconut shell. "The inscription is in ancient Euphorian, a dead language no longer spoken. Fortunately, I wrote a monograph last year on ancient tongues, including the Euphorian, so I'll translate from my notes. Silence, please—it's difficult work."

Pen in paw, he bent over his notebook, oblivious to everything but the task he had set himself.

An hour later he looked up. "The second clue is here—we are three days' sail from the Island of Pygmy Cats. But before we leave this cliff, I'd like to read the inscription aloud."

As we listened, the long-dead mouse king came alive again in all his glory:

I, ELYOD OF EUPHORIA, DECREED THAT
ON THIS CLIFF MY WORDS BE CARVED.
KNOW YE THAT I PERISHED NOT AT SEA.
THERE CAME A STORM, A WILD AND
WILLFUL THING! IT WRECKED OUR SHIP

BUT SPARED OUR LIVES, CASTING US ASHORE TO BUILD OUR LIVES ANEW.

UPON THE ISLE WERE PYGMY CATS AS SMALL AS MICE, DWELLING IN CAVES, WORSHIPPING MANY GODS AND GODDESSES. WE WORSHIP ONLY ONE, THE GODDESS ELOTANA. THE CAVECATS MARVELED AT OUR ARTS AND LEARNING. ERE LONG, THEY BEGGED THAT I BECOME THEIR KING.

I, ELYOD OF EUPHORIA, REIGN OVER MICE AND PYGMY CATS, ALL EQUAL IN MY EYES, UPON AN ISLE BUT THREE DAYS' SAIL FROM HERE.

YE WHO READ THESE WORDS—TOUCH NOT, SPOIL NOT THESE WRITINGS HEWN IN ROCK! MY DEEDS MUST BE REMEMBERED FOR ETERNITY.

As Basil's voice died away, we bowed our heads in silent homage to King Elyod.

10

The Island of Kataarh

Westward bound, the *Rosetta* set sail in the pink and purple and gold of a tropical sunset. Viewing the splendor outspread in the sky, I reflected that neither mice nor men could equal Nature's handiwork.

Upon our return to the yacht, Basil had conferred with Captain Black, poring over dozens of maps and charts in an effort to find the right island.

At last Basil pointed to a tiny speck on an ocean chart, saying, "Captain, you've not mentioned this one, the Island of Kataarh. How far away is it?"

"Basil, it's so small that I overlooked it. Kataarh is two or three days' sail from here. I've never visited it, nor have any mouse captains I know—it's much too far off the regular shipping lanes. No one bothers to go there."

"The sailing-time is right," said Basil, "and the island is unknown. I have a hunch that it's the one we seek. Let's get under way."

Up came the anchor, and off we sailed.

At Basil's suggestion we borrowed archeology books from the ship's library, since we'd soon be having a go at ancient ruins.

Sprawled in deck chairs, our noses buried in the books, we studied the how and why of digging. We read of amateurs who excavated heedlessly, destroying valuable objects that could never be replaced. We read enough to have a rough idea of digging techniques.

At noon of the third day a seamouse

perched high in the rigging shouted, "Land ho!"

Eagerly we rushed to the rail for our first glimpse of the hauntingly lovely Island of Kataarh.

I tingled with excitement, feeling much as Columbus must have felt when at last he sighted land—this, too, marked the end of a long quest.

The *Rosetta* moved slowly into a sheltered bay and dropped anchor. Leaving only a skeleton crew aboard, several boatloads of us rowed toward the beach.

We could see gentle waves lapping at white

sands, tall, slender palm trees, low hills and rich green valleys. High above all loomed a sleeping volcano, its slopes thick with trees.

"Truly an island paradise!" declared Lord Adrian.

We beached the boats and went ashore. There we pitched tents, filled our water jugs at a river, and dined on bread, cheese, and coconut milk.

The full tropical moon smiled down upon us, and we felt glad to be on land again.

Before we went to sleep, Basil had some words of caution for us. "Don't go looking for pygmy cats tomorrow, or for Elyod's descendants, if any. We don't want to frighten them away. This isle is so isolated that the creatures who live here now may be primitive and superstitious, afraid of strangers. Don't seek them out—let them come to us of their own free will. Good night, all!"

We retired to our tents. No pygmy cats interrupted our slumbers.

11

We Dig!

We awakened early the next day and breakfasted on tasty tropical fruits.

Basil had decided to begin digging.

"We'll put our time to good use while we are waiting for the pygmy cats to show themselves. What happened here on Kataarh, so long ago? To learn the answer, we excavate! Our shovels and spades will dig up ancient history. Come along, and make as much noise as you like, so the pygmy cats can hide if they fear us. I'll walk ahead, like the Pied Piper, playing my flute."

Carrying tools and small ladders, we followed our leader, who kept peering through a spyglass.

"I'm looking for mouse-made mounds, not natural ones," he explained. "Under these mounds are the ruins of the past. After the grass grows, men and mice always build anew, over the ruins of the old."

He peered through his spyglass. "Ah! I see a mound at the foot of the volcano that seems to be mouse-made. We'd best investigate."

We hurried after him. The mound was low, with a growth of grass and ferns, and looked like a large round table with a slight rise at the center.

Basil studied the rise for several minutes.

Then he rose and said, "Here we dig!"

"What made you decide the mound was mouse-made?" asked Tillary Quinn.

"I noticed that the grass on the mound

grows evenly and thickly everywhere but at
the center. There it's thin and patchy, which
is not Mother Nature's way. I deduced that
the mound must be mouse-made. When we
dig, we'll learn what's beneath the rise."

He told each of us where to begin digging,
and we went to work.

Two hours went by, then three. We kept
at it. Our spades turned up nothing but black
volcanic soil, even though the trench we had
dug was now waist deep. Basil stood up
above, directing us.

Suddenly my shovel scraped against a hard
object.

"Basil!" I shouted. "I've struck something!"

He jumped into the trench and told us all
to dig carefully at that spot, so as not to
damage whatever lay beneath."

Gradually our shovels uncovered something
which we soon saw was the top of a gigantic
marble head. Excitedly we dug deeper. Next
we beheld enormous eyes, a tilted nose, and
smiling lips.

"It's Elotana, Goddess of Goodness!" I cried.

We stood in the trench looking in awe and wonderment at the beautiful head sculptured in creamy marble. Elotana had always been the supreme god-figure in ancient Euphoria. Here was proof positive that Euphorian mice had come to Kataarh. Our work would fill many blank pages of mouse history, and I felt proud yet humble to be part of it all.

Basil echoed my thoughts. "My friends, exciting discoveries are waiting to be made! The world of mice will long remember what we do here. Look at this head—the perfectly formed lips, the lifelike appearance. It's a work of art, of classic Euphorian design, with just a trace of the Oriental. Elyod maintained his own high artistic standards on this remote isle. I am certain he bettered the lot of the pygmy cats he found here, taught them to read and write and enriched their lives. How sad that a volcanic eruption destroyed everything!"

"Are you certain of this?" asked Julian Wolff.

"Yes. Yonder volcano, sleeping now, became a fearful thing that spewed forth the

red-hot liquid rock called lava. Flowing down the slopes of the volcano, the lava dragged along with it earth and rocks and water. It poured down the mountain, covering every-

thing in its path. Thus was Elyod's city destroyed, buried under a river of lava and debris that crept on, filling fields, homes, the palace, until all was lost to view. When lava cools, it hardens and becomes solid, sealing off whatever is trapped underneath. Since that time other eruptions may have buried the city even more deeply. In Italy, where men excavate the buried cities of Pompeii and Herculaneum, more is learned about ancient times than ever was written in books. Here on Kataarh we mice shall dig down through the lava until a lost mouse city once more sees the light of day!"

Stirred by his dramatic words, we reached for our tools, but he put his paw to his lips for silence.

"We are not alone!" he whispered.

We turned around. Kneeling before the head of the mouse goddess were about thirty pygmy cats!

12

The Pygmy Cats

After journeying so far and waiting so long to see the pygmy cats, I must confess to disappointment.

The crude weapons beside them were typical of primitive cavecats—clubs, bows and arrows, stone axes. Some cats must have survived the volcanic eruption of Elyod's time, and these cats were their descendants. When they rose, I saw their faces.

Where were the alert, intelligent expressions of the pygmy cats on the golden goblet and on the vase? These cats looked dull-witted. Away from the civilizing influence of mice, the creatures had gone back to their barbaric ways.

Suddenly their leader pointed at Basil and began jabbering away to the others, who all nodded.

Then, to our utter amazement, all but the leader flung themselves to the ground and covered their eyes, purring happily. The leader marched over to my friend, bowed three times, and spoke in an unfamiliar language. Basil understood it, however, for he answered. We knew he had refused a request, for shaking one's head from side to side means *no* in any language.

Sadly the leader spoke to the cats on the ground, who stopped purring and began to weep and wail.

Basil explained matters. "Embarrassing, most embarrassing! These simple souls want me to be their king! The chief, Kahlúa the

78

Strong, says it was once foretold that a tall mouse with piercing eyes would one day come to rule them. I refused politely, having no wish to rule them or anyone."

"Ah, but you have such a kingly bearing!" jested Lord Adrian, and we all bowed low before Basil.

Kahlúa thought my friend had changed his mind about being king, and said something to the cats. They stopped wailing and began purring again.

Basil frowned. "Now you've confused the poor things! They do speak ancient Euphorian, but right there ends any resemblance to Elyod's brilliant cats of bygone days. Without mice to guide them, the pygmy cats accomplished nothing, for they are of low intelligence."

A long talk with Kahlúa then took place, at the end of which Basil looked pleased.

"The Chief promises that the cats will not interfere with our digging, because they believe me to be their king, and a king can do no wrong. However, they are superstitious about disturbing the ground. They still worship gods and goddesses—the one they fear most is the God of the Smoking Mountain. They say he lives deep down in the volcano. Elotana, Goddess of Goodness, is loved the best."

He led us back to the digs, saying, "Our

main trench runs from east to west. Now we'll cross it with one going north to south, after which I shall decide about minor trenches. Dig, friends, dig!"

So we dug, from morn 'til noon 'til night! In true British tradition we stopped for tea each afternoon. Even the American, Young Richard, grew to cherish the happy hours over the teacups.

The pygmy cats watched us curiously. We were amused to see them fall down and cover their faces whenever Basil walked toward them. They believed that only their chief was worthy enough to see a king's face. They rose after Basil passed, but if he turned his head, down they went! He protested to Kahlúa, but the cats continued their homage.

On the fourth day we unearthed a stone building. Basil translated an inscription on the front:

THE HALL OF THE LAWMAKERS

The roof had caved in under the heavy lava. We removed the debris, which the sailors carted off in wheelbarrows. We hollowed out the main chamber. Pillars supported a gallery for spectators. Below were white marble benches and a platform. One almost expected the lawmakers to enter!

We excavated many other buildings—a theater, temples, a stadium, a library. The theater seats were hewn of rock, with the stage far below. The city was built around a great square, with Elotana's statue in the center.

In a tent used as a storeroom Basil classified and tagged objects of art. Then sailors rowed the relics out to the *Rosetta* for safekeeping.

Elyod's palace was of classic beauty, inside and out. The architect's name was on the cornerstone—Sudipal Sirrom, a mouse of true genius.

The palace held enough works of art to fill a dozen museums—vases, figurines, golden goblets, armchairs of silver and gold, bowls of alabaster, jade ornaments, and beautiful sculpture. There were also bathtubs and a drainage system that would do credit to the mouse engineers of today.

Wall paintings appeared fresh and new, their colors bright and vivid against pale yellow backgrounds.

In one room a magnificent golden throne dazzled our eyes. A wall painting showed pygmy cats proudly carrying Elyod and his queen in bamboo chairs that trailed flowers. Another showed a parade of mouse and cat athletes. In a third, mouse lawmakers sat in session while cats listened from the gallery.

The fourth wall showed a banquet scene. King Elyod and Queen Nairda and guests sat at a long table. Next to Elyod was a handsome mouse, probably Semloh the Poet Prince, who had left Euphoria as a boy. Smiling pygmy cats served the guests, each bearing a golden platter heaped high with cheese.

Chief Kahlúa pointed out the remarkable resemblance between Basil and Semloh. We

too, were amazed—the detective and the prince were both tall and thin, with hawklike profiles and deep-set eyes.

Kahlúa approached Basil and spoke earnestly for a few minutes. Naturally, we did not understand his words, but Basil did.

Nodding vigorously to the cat, he turned toward us, saying, "This is news indeed! Kahlúa will lead, and we will follow. Our destination is a cave high on a hill. There, my friends, I confidently expect to make a most important archeological discovery, one that will astound mouse scholars and scientists— the Semloh Scrolls!"

"But I've never heard of the Semloh Scrolls," said Tillary Quinn.

"Precisely the point, my dear Australian. Nor has anyone else, but the mouse world will soon be talking of nothing *but* the Semloh Scrolls!"

13

The Semloh Scrolls

Within a half hour we were plodding up a hill at the other end of the island, on a winding path that led to the caves of the pygmy cats.

Many of them peeped out of their caves to see who was coming, and when they saw Basil, flung themselves down as usual, eyes covered, remaining on the ground until he had passed. They were still convinced that the mouse detective was their long-awaited king.

The Chief's cave was the highest on the hill. We followed him inside and helped him remove a large flat stone from the rear wall. Through the opening we entered a smaller cave, where stood an enormous jar, as tall as ourselves. I held a lantern for Basil while he read the writing on the jar.

"Incredible!" cried he. "In this jar are

scrolls that tell of Elyod's wanderings since he left his native land. Kahlúa, who cannot read, says that the jar has always stood here, even in his grandfather's time, but he'll allow us to remove it."

Enlarging the opening, we eased the heavy jar through. Getting it downhill was difficult, but it finally stood in Basil's tent, undamaged.

"Pray excuse me," said he. "I wish to translate some of the scrolls. I must place them under glass, lest they tear or crumple, and prefer to be alone for this delicate task. Meanwhile, it might be a good idea for Young Richard to make a map of the island."

So saying, Basil vanished into his tent.

We watched Richard draw a large map showing bays, beaches, lakes, the volcano, and other geographical features. Then we discussed place-names, which led to much merriment.

Tillary Quinn, our Australian, said, there's a place in New Zealand the Maoris call TAUMATAWHAKATANGIHANGAKOAVAVO-

TAMATEAPOKAIWHENUAKITANATAHU. Fifty-seven letters—it must be the world's longest name."

"Ah, but you're wrong," exclaimed Lord Adrian. "There's a charming village in Wales. It's called LLANFAIRPWLLGWYNGYLLGOGERY-CHWYRNDRDBWLLLLANDYSILIAGOGOGACH. Fifty-eight letters!"

"Well!" said Richard. "In America we have short Indian names. In Massachusetts there's CHARGOGGAGOGGMANCHAUGAGOGG-CHAUBUNAGUNGAMAUGG, in New York MAN-HANSICHAHAQUASHAWAMUCH, and in New Hampshire QUOQUINAPASSAKESSANANNA-QUAG."

It was some time before we could stop laughing.

"Canada has a town called PUNKEYDOO-DLES CORNER," said Dr. Wolff.

"Australia has WAGGA WAGGA!" said Tillary.

"And America has WALLA WALLA!" said Richard.

"How about our own names?" I asked.

"BASIL BAY? STARRETTI STREET? ADRIAN AVENUE? Let's vote!"

We wrote down our choices. When the votes were counted, Young Richard printed the winning names on the map.

Surprisingly, only one long name won. The rest were—see for yourself! I reproduce the completed map, an odd one indeed:

The map sent us off into gales of laughter.

"Mice will be mice!" cried Cherbou, and

PIMIENTO POINT

CREAM CHEESE CHANNEL

LIEDERKRANZ LAGOON

LAKE LIMBURGER

•EAST EDAM

◉ CAMP CHEDDAR

GULF OF GOUDA

GULF OF GRUYÈRE

PORT SALUT

CAPE CAMEMBERT

ROQUEFORT RIVER

MT. KATAARH

PROVOLONE POND

GULF OF GORGONZOLA

BAY OF BRIE

STRAITS OF SBRINZ

BLEU BEACH

PT. PARMESAN

CAPE OF CHARGOGGAGOGGMANCHAUGA-
GOGGCHAUBUNAGUNGAMAUGG

then our gay mood changed, for Basil appeared and spoke to us in a voice filled with emotion.

"I have read the first two scrolls and the last," he said. "Semloh was not only a great poet but a historian and a philosopher.

"The first scroll tells how the Euphorians were royally received by Far Eastern mice. They sailed for home, their ship laden with rare spices and exotic Oriental cheeses. The second scroll describes the storm that cast them upon Kataarh. The pygmy cats welcomed them. They had never seen mice before Elyod came. All lived happily together."

He paused, his eyes somber. "The last scroll is a long epic poem. Only the literary mice of London could do justice to Semloh's poetic gifts. With apologies for my poor translation, I will read the closing lines, the last he ever wrote:

Now all is calm, and I can scarce believe
That yesterday a rain of ash and fire

From yon volcano poured. All fled in
    fear
And on the shore sought refuge in
    canoes.
We paddled far, and from the blue-green
    sea
Saw fiery lava pouring down the slopes,

A stream that ever widened, flowing fast,
And in its path our beauteous city stood!
Then suddenly the stream of lava slowed
And halted just before the city gates.
So did the dread volcano spare us all.

Yet there's a tale oft told by pygmy cats.
Two angry gods fought fiercely, night
    and day—
The god who in the great volcano dwells
And he who rules the waters of the sea.
One spat forth flame and lava, fiery-hot,
The other sent high waves across the isle,
And all who lived there perished! None
    escaped,
Save for some pygmy cats high on a hill.

*Today the monster sleeps, but when it
    wakes,*
*Will none of us survive, will naught
    remain?*
I tremble at the thought of what may be!
*My scrolls! I'll store them in a hillside
    cave*
*Far from the feared volcano! This I
    vow—*
*Should this fair isle be one day lost to
    view,*
My royal father shall not be forgot—
*The Semloh Scrolls shall tell his deathless
    deeds.*

Thus, I reflected, had Elyod's story ended
—the Euphorian mice had all been victims
of the volcano.

But I had no time for further thought—
there was an ominous rumbling sound, and
the earth shook.

"The volcano has awakened!" cried Basil.

14

Volcano!

We stared up in fright at the volcano. From its cone a thin stream of smoke spiraled upward. The rumbling sounds stopped, and all was quiet.

"There's no reason for panic," said Basil. "From all I've read about volcanic eruptions, those were just preliminary rumbles. We've ample time for transporting ourselves and our belongings to the safety of the yacht. All the valuable objects we found are already aboard ship, except for the jar with the scrolls. I'll have the sailors attend to that immediately. I'll also tell them to bring back all the lifeboats—we'll need them."

Silently we went about the business of taking down the tents and packing our food and equipment.

From time to time the volcano rumbled, but Basil's presence calmed us as we loaded the boats. He had brought us safely through many perils before.

The boats went back and forth until everything was safely aboard the yacht. The others piled into a boat, and Basil and I were alone on the beach.

"The sailors will return for us in ten minutes," he said, and frowned. "Heavens! Where are the pygmy cats? They completely escaped my mind!"

We looked at the volcano. Toiling up the slope were the cats, with Kahlúa leading them.

"It's certain death to go up there!" cried

Basil, and screamed Kahlúa's name as we raced along.

The sky darkened. An enormous dust cloud

hovered over the volcano, almost hiding the sun.

Kahlúa walked back to meet us. The talk

was in Euphorian, but Basil later told me what was said. I write it in English for the reader's benefit.

Kahlúa said, "The God of the Smoking

Mountain is angered! He demands a sacrifice! Ten of us must leap into the flaming volcano.

Only then will he spare our beloved island. Farewell!"

And he ran back to lead the cats upward again.

"Now or never!" said Basil to me. "If it's a king they want, they shall have one, a king who will tell them fibs to save their lives!"

He darted ahead to face the cats. They fell to the ground, covering their faces.

"I am your king! Heed my words!" cried Basil. "Last night the God of the Smoking Mountain came to me in a dream. 'I do not want any more sacrifices,' he told me. 'Take the cats far away on your ship, for tomorrow I shall destroy this island!'"

Kahlúa trembled. "I did not know of your dream."

"Obey your king," said Basil sternly. "All must go to the beach. And tell your cats that it is no longer forbidden to look at a king's face."

We left none too soon, for a heavy rain began to fall, accompanied by thunder and lightning.

Basil and I and the thirty cats crowded into the lifeboat and were rowed out to the *Rosetta.*

Captain Black got under way at once, in surging, swelling seas. Only when we had reached calmer waters did we look back at the volcano.

We saw spectacular fireworks, a dazzling display of the monster's might! Flashes of

lightning illumined the inky darkness. From the cone of the volcano came showers of sparks, red and yellow and orange, swirling high in the air.

The sounds were deafening, as though a thousand cannons were firing away!

Tons of lava flowed down the slopes in a stream a mile wide. As more rain fell, the lava mixed with mud. Like a boiling lake the fiery-hot mass advanced upon the island.

"Kataarh is doomed!" cried Basil, and he was right.

The lava flowed over everything, even the hills. Clouds of hissing steam arose as the boiling lava entered the sea, but the sea was the final victor, for the lava vanished into its depths.

15

The Ten-Day Truce

When the *Rosetta* sailed into Bengistan Bay, thousands of cheering mice jammed the docks.

At a banquet that evening the Prime Minister delivered a stirring speech in which Basil was given the Mousterian Medal, the highest award in the land, and made an honorary citizen of Bengistan.

General Garmize spoke. He said that Bengistan now had the best-trained army in the world, and would never again fall prey to rats like Ratigan.

The Maharajah spoke last. By rights, all the valuable relics belonged to Bengistan, the mouse kingdom nearest Kataarh. Besides, the Maharajah had equipped our expedition and lent us the yacht.

But the Maharajah said, "Basil, one half of the antiquities you discovered will go to the museum closest to your heart—the British Mousmopolitan. As for the other valuable relics, I'll sell some to museums of other lands, for there is much poverty among my subjects. I'll tear down slums, build homes, schools, libraries, and good roads. A great many things of Elyod's time will be housed in our own museums. When mouse scientists from abroad come here to study the antiquities, Bengistan will become a center of learning and art."

Basil rose and shook the Maharajah's paw.

"For your generous gesture I thank you, and in the same breath ask a favor. What of the pygmy cats? I could bring them to London, where every mouse will want to get a glimpse of them. But they'd be unhappy, like animals in a zoo, always on display. Away from the tropical climate they are used to, they might become ill. Could you possibly—"

The Maharajah beamed. "Say no more, Basil! There's a private park on one of my estates. I'll have it fenced in, on top as well as on the sides, lest larger animals try to enter and harm them."

Thus was the fate of the pygmy cats decided, most happily for all concerned. Later, letters from the Maharajah told how wonderfully content the cats were. They had even asked for a teacher so that they could learn to read and write.

As for ourselves, we returned to London, where honors were heaped upon our heads —awards, conferences, banquets, scientific meetings. Basil, the center of all the ado, was elected president of the Royal Academy of Mouse Orientalists.

On the way home from the Academy dinner, Basil exclaimed, "Dawson! Why did I not think of it before now? The cats, the cats!"

"Pygmy cats?" I asked.

"No indeed. British cats!"

He would say no more, much as I questioned him, but a week later he announced *The Ten-Day Truce!*

He had asked himself who else besides

mice would wish to know about the pygmy cats. The answer was crystal clear.

Through Cyril the Stoolpigeon, Basil made contact with the leading cat scientists of Britain, inviting them to a series of lectures he planned to give.

Subject—the pygmy cats once ruled by mice.

Place—Rockhenge, the ancient mouse ruins he himself had discovered and excavated.

Terms—for the ten days of the lectures, no British cat was to catch, kill or eat a British mouse.

The cats accepted, and the famous ten-day truce began, an achievement that has never been equaled.

What peace and goodwill among cats and mice—smiles, paws waved in greeting, friendly little chats! It was a fine, good feeling.

The lectures were a huge success. While it was true that Lord Adrian and I quailed when the audience of cats crowded around to congratulate Basil after the last brilliant lecture, we needn't have worried.

Basil had chosen Rockhenge for a most practical reason—he knew the site well. There were plenty of holes to hide in, and every mouse attending the lectures was given a detailed diagram.

Kitty Milkington, a cat biologist, said to Basil, "I've thoroughly enjoyed your talks, and the truce, too. Perhaps there'll be another truce soon."

"Very soon, I hope," said Sir Thomas Catsworth.

Basil nodded. "I quite agree. But my next case will take me out of England, all the way to Mexico."

"Best of luck!" said the cats, and departed.

"Why didn't you tell me about the Mexican case?" I asked.

Basil of Baker Street smiled. "My dear doctor, that's another tale!"

29324 MISHMASH, by Molly Cone. Illustrated by Leonard Shortall. Life is full of surprises for Pete when he gets Mishmash—a huge, black, friendly hound who turns the whole town topsy-turvy with his hilarious doings. (60¢)

29322 THE STREET OF THE FLOWER BOXES, by Peggy Mann. Illustrated by Pete Burchard. When Carlos decides to launch a campaign to sell window boxes, he becomes the center of all kinds of activities on his block. (60¢)

29309 DANNY DUNN *and the Smallifying Machine,* by Jay Williams and Raymond Abrashkin. Illustrated by Paul Sagsoorian. When Danny gets trapped in Professor Bullfinch's latest invention, he shrinks to insect size and must face survival in a world that has become a giant jungle. (60¢)

29527 THE MYSTERIOUS BENDER BONES, by Susan Meyers. Illustrated by Ib Ohlsson. When Kermit and Brian are hired to do a peculiar "odd job" on Bender Island, they get tangled up with a mysterious stranger in a wild and hilarious search for treasure. (75¢)

29334 GERTRUDE KLOPPENBERG (Private), by Ruth Hooker. Illustrated by Gloria Kamen. Trudy confides to her diary all her most private thoughts and feelings about the ups and downs in her life. (60¢)

29510 MAPLE STREET, by Nan Hayden Agle. Illustrated by Leonora E. Prince. Margaret Gage launches a campaign to have an ugly vacant lot made into a playground with swings, seesaws, grass, and flowers. (75¢)

29333 ENCYCLOPEDIA BROWN TRACKS THEM DOWN, by Donald J. Sobol. Illustrated by Leonard Shortall. See if you can keep pace with America's favorite super-sleuth as he tackles ten more hard-to-solve cases. (60¢)

29543 THE GHOST NEXT DOOR, by Wylly Folk St. John. Illustrated by Trina Schart Hyman. Strange signs of the existence of a ghost next door trigger the curiosity of Lindsey and Tammy who resolve to find out just what's happening. (75¢)

29323 NEXT DOOR TO XANADU, by Doris Orgel. Illustrated by Dale Payson. If she only had a best friend, Patricia was sure that she wouldn't care about being called Fatsy Patsy. Then a new girl moves into the apartment next door. (60¢)

29546 DRUGS AND YOU, by Arnold Madison. Illustrated with photographs. This straightforward account gives you basic information about the use and abuse of today's major drugs. (75¢)

(If your bookseller does not have the titles you want, you may order them by sending the retail price, plus 25¢ for postage and handling to: Mail Service Department, POCKET BOOKS, a division of Simon & Schuster, Inc., 1 West 39th Street, New York, N. Y. 10018. Please enclose check or money order—do not send cash.)